MARY, QUEEN OF SCOTS

ESCAPE FROM LOCHLEVEN CASTLE

STORY BY
THERESA BRESLIN

ILLUSTRATIONS BY
TERESA MARTINEZ

Almost 500 years ago, in Linlithgow Palace near Edinburgh, King James V of Scotland and his French wife, Mary of Guise, had a baby girl. They named her Mary, like her mother.

Six days later, King James V died, and baby Mary, his only surviving child, was crowned Queen of Scotland.

Mary went to France, her mother's home country, to grow up safely with the French royal family. She spoke Scots and French and was taught other languages, music, horse riding, falconry and needlework. She married a French prince, and when she was just seventeen she became Queen of France as well as Queen of Scotland.

But soon after, Mary's husband, the French King, and her mother both died. In 1561, when she was eighteen, Mary returned to rule over Scotland. She married her cousin at Holyrood Palace in Edinburgh and had a baby, who was named James, after his grandfather.

Some of the Scottish lords wanted to control Mary and were jealous of the power gained by anyone she married. Her husband was killed, and the next man she married had to flee Scotland. Mary was captured by these rebel lords and taken to Sir William Douglas's island castle in the middle of Loch Leven, near Kinross.

Mary was trapped on the island, along with one loyal companion, Lady Seton. She was not allowed to rule Scotland or speak to her people. She could not see her baby son, meet her friends or ride her horse. As days, and then months went by, her hopes of rescue faded.

On a tiny island in the middle of Loch Leven there is a castle.

The only way to reach the castle is by boat.

Many years ago, in that castle on the island, a beautiful young queen was held prisoner.

Her name was Mary, Queen of Scots.

One spring morning, Queen Mary was especially unhappy. "Soon it will be May," she said, and a tear trickled down her cheek. "There will be games and celebrations, and yet I cannot escape Sir William Douglas, nor leave this island to be with my child and my friends."

"Come, Your Grace," Lady Seton said gently. "Don't forget that my brother George promised he would try to help you. Now, here is your best dress. I will curl your glorious red hair and put a ruff of fine lace around your neck. We will walk in the courtyard and see the preparations for May Day."

When Queen Mary and Lady Seton entered the courtyard, the pageboy of the castle was arranging flowers in a basket.

"Those are so pretty," said Mary.

The pageboy, who was named after Sir William but was always called Will, bowed low. "I chose them to please your Grace."

"I thank you," Mary replied in her sweet voice. "And look! My pet linnet has flown down to see them too."

Suddenly there was a loud squawk
and a flurry of feathers.
Mary screamed.
A cat had pounced upon the bird!

Will leaped forward and grabbed the cat.

The bird flew up to the castle wall.

"Such bravery!" Mary exclaimed, and the young lad's face glowed in delight. "But, you are wounded."

Using her own handkerchief, embroidered with an M, the Queen bound Will's arm.

"If only I was like my linnet," Mary sighed, "I might wing my way over the water and be free."

"One does not need wings to cross Loch Leven," Will replied slowly. "*I* can row a boat."

Mary's eyes opened wide with hope. But she also feared for the young lad. "Your uncle would punish you harshly," she said. "Do not place yourself in danger for my sake, Will Douglas."

That evening, like every evening, Sir William Douglas inspected Mary's room for any signs she might be trying to escape. He checked the food tray, her wardrobe and the hamper of clean laundry that was delivered daily.

Then, choosing a key from the bunch he always carried, he locked her door from the outside.

"Sir William keeps the castle keys always near him," Mary said to Lady Seton. "Neither young Will nor your brother George can rescue me. We are too well guarded!"

The next day the two ladies went for a walk around the little island. As they passed the castle washerwomen, one of them pressed a note into Lady Seton's hand.

"It is from my brother George!" the loyal lady whispered to the Queen.

"He says that from the first day of May he will wait each night on the opposite shore of Loch Leven to take you away."

"But I cannot swim," Mary cried out in despair, "so how will I reach the other side of the loch?"

The first day of May arrived and the castle was filled with music and feasting. Sir William and his relatives attended the party. But Mary missed her own family so much that she wanted to go early to bed. As she rose from the table, Will murmured, "George Seton is waiting. I will send you a signal."

All night, and throughout the next day, Queen Mary and Lady Seton were in a fever of anxiety. What would the signal be? When would it come?

That evening, Mary's jailor again checked her tray and wardrobe. As he bent to the laundry hamper, Sir William looked out the window. "What is that pageboy, Will, doing?" he snapped in annoyance. "Fiddling about with boats when he should be fetching my supper!"

A boat! Mary thought quickly. Could it possibly be for her? Her heart beat faster. As Sir William reached to open the window, she gasped: "Ah! I am faint!"

"I am sure you will recover once you eat your supper," was his curt reply. "I am going to eat mine."

As Sir William locked the door behind him, Lady Seton turned to Mary with concern, but the Queen said quietly: "I only pretended illness to distract our jailor's attention in case Will has a plan. But has he? So many hours have passed since he said he would send a signal." Her voice was strained.

"Maybe there is a message among the supper things." Lady Seton examined the dishes.

There was no message.

Then Mary knelt by the hamper of clean linen. She pushed aside the top sheet.

"Oh," she said, "a washerwoman has left her clothes here." She lifted out a homespun dress, a white hat and wooden clogs.

"Perhaps you are meant to wear them," said Lady Seton. "Is there a note?"

Mary searched in the hamper.

At the bottom lay a handkerchief. A blood-stained handkerchief. Mary lifted it out. It had the letter *M* embroidered on it.

The signal!

Lady Seton helped Mary put on the washerwoman's clothes, and she herself put on Mary's dress, saying, "If I stand by the window, anyone who glances up will think you are here."

They could see into the study of Sir William Douglas, where young Will was serving him supper. The castle keys lay on the table. Will filled his master's wine glass again and again. Sir William yawned and his head sank onto his chest.

Will dropped a napkin over the keys. Then, in one smooth movement, the boy lifted napkin and keys together and ran.

Within seconds Will was outside the Queen's room. The key grated in the lock.

"Quickly, Your Grace!" he urged. "Not a moment to lose!"

Mary hurried downstairs, through the opened castle gate…

…and stepped into a waiting boat.

Will set a course over the water and pulled hard
on the oars.

On the far shore stood Lady Seton's brother, George, with fast horses.

"Find another mount!" commanded Mary. "Will Douglas is coming with us. For this day he has loyally served Scotland and her Queen."

Taking one last look at the island castle of Loch Leven, Mary, Queen of Scots, galloped off to freedom.

Word spread that Mary had escaped, and the people cheered as she rode through towns.

At Langside, which is now part of Glasgow, her army fought the rebel Scottish lords. Mary lost the battle, but she escaped again, crossing the Solway Firth into England to ask her cousin, Queen Elizabeth I, for help to regain her throne.

However, Elizabeth was worried that Mary would claim the English throne. For eighteen years she held Mary captive in castles far from London, Scotland and the sea. Finally, convinced that her cousin was plotting against her, she signed the warrant for Mary's death.

Faithful Will Douglas remained in service with Mary to the end.

In 1587 Queen Mary went calmly and bravely to her death.

Mary's son James inherited her throne, and later also Elizabeth's. This united the two crowns, which was the beginning of today's United Kingdom.

Nowadays a ferryboat will take you across the water
to visit the ruined island castle of Loch Leven.